A Tiger for Breakfast

NARINDER DHAMI

ILLUSTRATED BY CHRISTOPHER CORR

BLOOMSBURY EDUCATION

BLOOMSBURY EDUCATION
Bloomsbury Publishing Plc
50 Bedford Square, London, WC1B 3DP, UK

BLOOMSBURY, BLOOMSBURY EDUCATION and the Diana logo are trademarks of
Bloomsbury Publishing Plc

First published in Great Britain in 2011 by A & C Black, an imprint of Bloomsbury Publishing Plc
This edition published in Great Britain in 2019 by Bloomsbury Publishing Plc
Text copyright © Narinder Dhami, 2011
Illustrations copyright © Christopher Corr, 2011

A catalogue record for this book is available from the British Library

ISBN: PB: 978-1-4729-5958-4 ; ePDF: 978-1-4729-5957-7; ePub: 978-1-4729-5956-0;
enhanced ePub: 978-1-4729-6946-0

2 4 6 8 10 9 7 5 3 1 (paperback)

Printed and bound in China by Leo Paper Products, Heshan, Guangdong

To find out more about our authors and books visit www.bloomsbury.com
and sign up for our newsletters

Chapter One

It was a hot, dusty day in India. The sun shone down on the flat green fields and the sky was blue.
Ram the farmer was digging his field.

Suddenly, a tiger jumped out of the trees. "My name is Bali," it said. "And I'm very, *very* hungry. So now I'm going to eat you!"

"Please don't do that!" cried Ram.
"My wife has a pretty white cow at
home. It will taste much better than me."

"Then bring me that cow," growled Bali. "And if you don't, I'll eat you, your wife and all your children!"

Chapter Two

Ram ran home
as fast as he could.

His wife Reeta was in the yard. She was milking the pretty white cow.

Ram told Reeta what had happened.

Reeta was very angry.
"You want me to give my pretty white cow to that greedy tiger?" she said. "Never!"

"But if I don't, Bali will eat you and me
and all our children!" said Ram.

"We'll see about that!" said Reeta.
She told Ram to go and get their horse.
But when he returned, Reeta had gone.

Chapter Three

Instead, there was a man in the yard.
Ram looked puzzled.

"Don't worry, Ram. It's only me!" laughed Reeta. "I'm wearing your turban and your clothes."

"Why are you doing that?" asked Ram.
"You'll see!" Reeta replied.

She got on the horse and rode out to the field.

Ram and the
pretty white cow
came with them.

"I hope I find a tiger today," Reeta said loudly. "I haven't eaten a tiger for days. And I do love a tiger for breakfast!"

Chapter Four

When Bali heard the farmer's wife, he was very frightened. He ran off into the forest to hide.

There, he bumped into a tiger called
Tikkoo.

"Hey," Tikkoo growled. "Look where
you're going!"

"Run!" Bali shouted. "That man in the field eats tigers for breakfast!"

Tikkoo peeped through the trees. He saw Reeta sitting on her horse.

"You fool," Tikkoo laughed. "That is the farmer's wife dressed like a man. Now, let's go and eat *them* for breakfast!"

23

"How do I know you are telling the truth?" Bali asked. "What if you run off and leave me?"

"We'll tie our tails together," said
Tikkoo. "Then I can't go anywhere
without you."
So that's what the tigers did.

Chapter Five

Ram and Reeta were laughing about
how they'd tricked Bali.

Suddenly, they saw *two* tigers run out of the trees.

"That's Tikkoo, the biggest tiger in the land!" said Ram. He was very frightened.

"Hello, Tikkoo, my friend," called
Reeta. "I see you've brought Bali for
my breakfast. He's a nice fat tiger, and
I'm *so* hungry. You can have my pretty
white cow in return!"

Bali looked at Tikkoo. "You tricked me," he growled.

"No, I didn't," said Tikkoo. "She's lying!"

But Bali wouldn't listen.
He ran off into the forest,
pulling Tikkoo with him.

Reeta and Ram laughed. Then they went home with their pretty white cow.